W9-CNJ-555

PETS I WOULDN'T PICK

To librarians, parents, and teachers:

Pets I Wouldn't Pick is a Parents Magazine READ ALOUD Original — one title in a series of colorfully illustrated and fun-to-read stories that young readers will be sure to come back to time and time again.

Now, in this special school and library edition of *Pets I Wouldn't Pick,* adults have an even greater opportunity to increase children's responsiveness to reading and learning — and to have fun every step of the way.

When you finish this story, check the special section at the back of the book. There you will find games, projects, things to talk about, and other educational activities designed to make reading enjoyable by giving children and adults a chance to play together, work together, and talk over the story they have just read.

Parents Magazine READ ALOUD Originals:

Golly Gump Swallowed a Fly
The Housekeeper's Dog
Who Put the Pepper in the Pot?
Those Terrible Toy-Breakers
The Ghost in Dobbs Diner
The Biggest Shadow in the Zoo
The Old Man and the Afternoon Cat
Septimus Bean and His Amazing Machine
Sherlock Chick's First Case
A Garden for Miss Mouse
Witches Four
Bread and Honey
Pigs in the House
Milk and Cookies
But No Elephants
No Carrots for Harry!
Snow Lion
Henry's Awful Mistake
The Fox with Cold Feet
Get Well, Clown-Arounds!
Pets I Wouldn't Pick
Sherlock Chick and the Giant Egg Mystery

Library of Congress Cataloging-in-Publication Data

Schmeltz, Susan Alton.
Pets I wouldn't pick / by Susan Alton Schmeltz; pictures by Ellen Appleby. — North American library ed.
p. cm. — (Parents magazine read aloud original)
Summary: Poetic pros and cons for a variety of pet possibilities including frogs, pigs, bats, and elephants.
ISBN 0-8368-0896-7
[1. Pets—Fiction. 2. Stories in rhyme.] I. Appleby, Ellen, ill. II. Title. III. Series.
PZ8.3.S364Pe 1993
[E]—dc20 92-32349

This North American library edition published in 1993 by Gareth Stevens Publishing, 1555 North RiverCenter Drive, Suite 201, Milwaukee, Wisconsin 53212, USA, under an arrangement with Parents Magazine Press, New York.

Printed in the United States of America

1 2 3 4 5 6 7 8 9 98 97 96 95 94 93

Pets I Wouldn't Pick

by Susan Alton Schmeltz
pictures by Ellen Appleby

Gareth Stevens Publishing • Milwaukee
Parents Magazine Press • New York

To P. and T.,
who keep me laughing — S.A.S.

For my father — E.A.

Choosing pets? Here's free advice:
Don't pick frogs and don't pick mice!

I don't think you'd like a frog.
Frogs don't sit like lumps on logs.
Count on frogs to hip and hop.
And they hardly *ever* stop!

On the counter, on the bed,
On the hat on Grandma's head!

Mice don't hop or jump or slink.
They just nap beneath the sink.
Or play games of hide and seek,
Scaring Sister when they peek.

So before you hear Mom shout,
Why not choose to leave mice out?

There are other pets, you know.
But to squirrels and pigs, say, "No!"

Squirrels are cute as they can be
When they jump from tree to tree.
But in the house a squirrel's a pest,
Hiding nuts and building nests.

What if Auntie comes to call
And trips on acorns in the hall?

Do you think you'd like a pig?
Round and pink and not too big?
What about the piggy's pen?
It won't fit in Daddy's den!

And where will you go to scrub
When pig's mud bath fills your tub?

I'm not through, now please take note:
Owls and bats don't get my vote.

True, an owl will talk to you,
But his only word is "WHOO."
And his feathers fill the air
As he flies from lamp to chair.

How much sleeping could you do
Knowing that he's watching you?

Friends of yours won't spend the night
If your bats give them a fright.
They won't like it when bats zoom
Out of closets in your room!

Bats, I'm sure you will agree,
Just don't fit your family.

Heed my word of warning please:
Don't take spiders! Don't take fleas!

Spiders don't know how to play.
They just spin their webs all day
From the ceiling to the floor,
On the mantle, out the door,

Down the chimney, up the stairs,
Trapping Brother in their snares!

As for fleas, I'm sure you know
They can put on quite a show.
But when the circus star's a flea,
He is hard for you to see.

So your neighbor's dog, Lamar,
Might just walk off with your star.

Two more pets that won't be missed:
Goats and moles, cross off your list!

Goats are good at eating cans.
But did you say you had plans
To get bumped on your back end
Every single time you bend?

You could wind up with your nose
Planted in a yellow rose!

Worst of all about the moles
Is their love of digging holes
In the garden, and the yard,
Making running rather hard.

They leave humps and lumpy hills,
Bringing Daddy gardening bills.

Honestly, here's how I feel:
Skip the beaver! Skip the seal!

Beavers are a busy bunch,
Working while you eat your lunch,
Chomping tables, chewing chairs,
Nibbling railings on the stairs.

Now what will the plumber think
Of those dams in all the sinks?

Your pet seal would make Mom wish
She could lock up every dish.
He will bounce them on his nose
Like the seals in juggling shows.

Get the dust pan! Get the broom!
Two more saucers just went BOOM!

Please be careful, please beware:
Not one elephant! Not one bear!

Elephants would be too hard
For you to squeeze into your yard.
If your bird bath was smashed flat,
You'd know where your pet just sat.

And his tummy's tough to fill.
Could you pay
the grocer's bill?

Honey is a bear's delight.
He can eat it noon or night.
In the winter, in your bed,
With Gramp's nightcap on his head,

Your big, sticky bear will snore,
Then in spring he'll eat some more!

Other pets you should resist
Follow on a handy list:

Alligators, crocodiles —
You can't trust their sneaky smiles.

Porcupines and buffalo —
Where you'd keep them, I don't know!

Walruses and chimpanzees.
Wasps, a hive of honey bees.

Hippos, mother kangaroos.
Aardvarks, eels, and baby gnus.

Whales, giraffes, koala bears.
Hedgehogs that roll down the stairs…

Whew! I'm tired, so could *you* list
Pesky pets that I have missed?

Because it's time for me to feed...

FRIDGE

My new pet octopus, McSneed!

Notes to Grown-ups

Major Themes

Here is a quick guide to the significant themes and concepts at work in *Pets I Wouldn't Pick:*

- Animal behavior: the animals are shown doing the kind of activities they usually do.
- The fun of seeing things in unexpected places: wild animals seem strange in ordinary homes.

Step-by-step Ideas for Reading and Talking

Here are some ideas for further creative discussion of *Pets I Wouldn't Pick* between grown-ups and children.

- This book is handy for filling in odd moments. There is no plot that has to be followed. Instead, each spread describes one kind of animal in words and pictures, so you and your child can read any one at a time.
- The pictures are filled with busy animals bouncing around the house behaving in the right way *for them*. The book asks if you can list any other pesky pets. You might also talk about the differences between wild animals and domesticated ones like dogs and cats.

How many animals can you name?

Learning Can Be Fun

Visiting the Pet Store

While the pets in this story are more trouble than most families are willing to put up with, knowing about animals is an important part of general knowledge that will help your child do well in school. A child who doesn't know a cat from a bat will have a harder time relating to them in stories than a child who knows a little something about these animals.

Often closer to your home than the zoo, a pet store is a great place to go just to visit the animals and get to know what they look like firsthand. Some stores have exotic birds and unusual animals in addition to the normal puppies, kittens, and guinea pigs. Admission to the stores is free, so you can "visit" as often as you like.

Before you visit a pet store, however, be sure you make it clear to your child that you are not going to buy an animal, unless you plan to let your child choose a certain kind of pet. If, on the other hand, you want to get your child started on the responsibility and fun of pet care, a small goldfish is a good place to start. It is inexpensive, fairly easy to care for, and does not cause allergic reactions to anyone. And then, buying more fish food will be a great excuse to stop back every month or so and see what new animals have arrived at the pet store.

About the Author

SUSAN ALTON SCHMELTZ picked a very unusual pet when she was little: a baby squirrel that her cat had found and brought home. Her mother decided the family could keep him until he grew big enough to go free.

About the Artist

ELLEN APPLEBY thinks hers is the most exceptional of pets: an Airedale named Nancy. Nancy understands more than 70 words, loves flute music, and enjoys singing along!

GUMDROP BOOKS - Bethany, Missouri